The Wind in the Willows

A DORLING KINDERSLEY BOOK

Produced by Leapfrog Press Ltd

Project Editor Naia Bray-Moffatt
Art Editor Penny Lamprell
Designers Catherine Goldsmith and Adrienne Hutchinson

For Dorling Kindersley
Senior Editor Marie Greenwood
Managing Art Editor Jacquie Gulliver
Picture Research Liz Moore
Production Joanne Rooke

First published in Great Britain in 2000 by Dorling Kindersley Limited
9 Henrietta Street, London WC2E 8PS
2 4 6 8 10 9 7 5 3 1
www.dk.com

Colour reproduction by Bright Arts, Hong Kong
Printed in Italy by L.E.G.O.
A CIP catalogue record for this book is available from the British Library.

Acknowledgements
The publisher would like to thank the following for their kind permission to reproduce their photographs:
a=above; c=centre; b=bottom; l=left; r=right; t=top

Bridgeman Art Library: 26, 46t, 48br; Bruce Coleman Collection: 46c, bl, br, 46-7, 47tl, cla, clb, bc, br, Mary Evans Picture
Library: 10tr, 17br, 23tr, 30, 33tr, 44b, 48cr; Ronald Grant Archive: 48bl;
Robert Harding Picture Library: 35t, 41t; Hulton Getty Images: 48tl; NHPA: 47cr
"Inventing Wonderland - The Live Fantasies of Lewis Carroll, Edward Lear, JM Barrie, Kenneth Grahame, AA Milne" by
Jackie Wallschläger © Charles Scribner, 1933 renewed 1961 by kind permission of Methuen Publishing Limited.

Young DK Classics

The Wind in the Willows

By **Kenneth Grahame**
Adapted by **Sally Grindley**

Illustrated by
Eric Copeland

DK

Dorling Kindersley

Contents

A Riverbank Map

HERE IS A MAP OF WHERE the animals you will meet in this story live. The story was written in 1908, but the riverbank described would look much the same today.

✸ TOAD HALL

Toad is very rich and lives in a grand country house with lawns that sweep down to the river.

✸ BADGER'S HOME

Badger lives in an underground home in the heart of the Wild Wood. Mole and Rat spend a happy evening here.

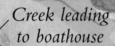

Creek leading to boathouse

Boathouse

This is the secret underground passage that leads from the riverbank into the middle of Toad Hall.

Here is the weir with a mill wheel and mill house that Mole and Rat pass on Mole's first boat trip down the river.

Rat and Mole enjoy a delicious picnic here by the river.

The Wide World

The Wild Wood

❋ THE WIDE WORLD
The Wide World is considered a dangerous place by most of the riverbank animals. Toad has some exciting adventures here.

❋ MOLE GETS LOST
Poor Mole has a frightening experience when he gets lost in the Wild Wood looking for Badger.

❋ RAT'S HOME
Rat lives in a hole in the riverbank itself.

The river

Rat's boat

❋ MOLE END
Mole is ashamed to show his shabby underground home to Rat. But Rat thinks it is "a delightful house ... so neat and well planned".

The Riverbank

At last, pop! his snout
came out into the sunlight.

MOLE HAD BEEN WORKING HARD all morning, spring-cleaning his little home. Now he had dust in his throat and eyes, splashes of whitewash all over his black fur, and O how his back and arms ached. Spring was in the air, and there was no escape from those strange feelings of longing and discontent that it brought. It was hardly surprising then that Mole suddenly flung his brush on the floor, said "Bother!" and "O blow!" and "Hang spring-cleaning!", bolted out of the house and made for the steep tunnel that led up above. He scraped and scratched and scrabbled and scrooged, working busily with his little paws and muttering, "Up we go! Up we go!" till at last, pop! his snout came out into the sunlight.

Mole found himself rolling in the soft grass of a great meadow. "O my, this is better than whitewashing!" he said as the sun warmed his fur and soft breezes stroked his whiskers. He set off across the meadow, skipping along in the joy of spring without its cleaning, until he reached the hedge on the far side.

Everywhere birds were building, flowers budding, leaves thrusting. Mole couldn't help but delight in being lazy while everyone else was so busy.

He thought his happiness was complete when suddenly he came to the edge of a swirling river. Never in his life had he seen a river before. Mole was bewitched, entranced, as he watched this sparkling, full-bodied animal, chasing and chuckling, gripping things with a gurgle and leaving them with a laugh. He trotted along by the side of it, then sat on the bank while the river chattered on to him, a babbling procession of the best stories in the world.

As he looked across the river at the opposite bank, he spotted a dark hole and began to dream about what a nice snug home it would make. Something small and bright seemed to twinkle deep inside. It vanished then twinkled again like a tiny star. Then, as he looked, it winked at him, and a small face appeared.

It was the Water Rat!

He thought his happiness was complete when suddenly he came to the edge of a swirling river.

"Hullo, Mole!" said the Water Rat.
"Hullo, Rat!" said Mole.
"Would you like to come over?"
"And how will I do that?" replied Mole rather sulkily.

Rat stepped into a little boat and rowed quickly across the river. Mole felt himself growing excited as he held on to Rat's paw and stepped gingerly down into the stern of the boat.

"I've never been in a boat before," he said as Rat pushed off from the bank.

"Never been in a –?" cried Rat in astonishment. "What have you been doing then?"

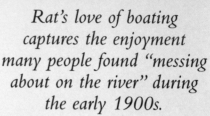

Rat's love of boating captures the enjoyment many people found "messing about on the river" during the early 1900s.

"Is it as nice as all that?" asked Mole shyly.

"It's the only thing," said Rat. "There is nothing – absolutely nothing - half as much worth doing as messing about in boats –"

"Look out, Rat!" cried Mole suddenly. But it was too late. The boat struck the bank and Rat lay on his back, his heels in the air! "Look here!" continued Rat, picking himself up with a smile. "If you've nothing else to do, why don't we row down the river together and make a long day of it?"

Mole waggled his toes from sheer happiness while Rat rowed over to his home to retrieve a huge hamper.

Mole was dizzy with the sparkle, the ripple, the smells, and the sounds of the river.

A little further on, Mole waved a paw towards an area of woodland and asked, "What lies over there?"

"O, that's the Wild Wood," said Rat shortly. "We riverbankers don't go there much. Dear Old Badger lives right in the heart of it; wouldn't live anywhere else if you paid him. But the weasels, stoats and foxes – sometimes they go a bit wild and you can't really trust them."

"And beyond the Wild Wood?"

"Is the Wide World," said Rat. "And that's something we don't talk about. Now if you're ready, it's time to stop and have lunch."

"There is nothing half as much worth doing as messing about in boats," said Rat.

"Can I unpack it by myself?" begged Mole, as Rat swung the hamper ashore. Rat was only too happy to oblige, and sprawled on the grass to rest. Mole gasped as he opened the mysterious packets one by one. "O my!" he exclaimed over and over, and tucked in hungrily when invited by Rat.

Many mouthfuls later, Mole looked up to see a broad wet snout poking up above the edge of the bank. It was Otter.

"Hello, Rat. Pleased to meet you, Mole. All the world seems to be out on the river today. I've just seen Toad, rolling all over the place in his brand new sculling-boat."

"Once, it was nothing but sailing," chuckled Rat. "Then punting. Last year, he was going to spend the rest of his life in a houseboat. It's all the same, whatever he takes up; he gets tired of it and starts on something fresh."

Just then, a mayfly hovered over the river. In a flash, Otter was gone, leaving nothing but a streak of bubbles on the surface.

The afternoon sun was sinking fast by the time Rat sculled dreamily homewards. Mole, very full of lunch and pleased with himself, thought how well he and boats were getting along. After a while he said, "Ratty! Please, I want to row!"

Rat shook his head. "It's not so easy as it looks," he smiled.

Mole's pride whispered that he could do it every bit as well. He jumped up and seized the sculls so suddenly that Rat fell backwards off his seat. The triumphant Mole took his place, while Rat cried from the bottom of the boat, "Stop it, you blockhead! You'll have us over!"

Mole flung his sculls back with a flourish, made a great dig at the water, missed, and landed on top of Rat. He tried to grab the side of the boat, and the next moment — over it went.

How cold the water was, and how very wet it felt. How welcome the sun looked to Mole when he rose spluttering to the surface, and how black his despair when he began to sink again. Then a firm paw

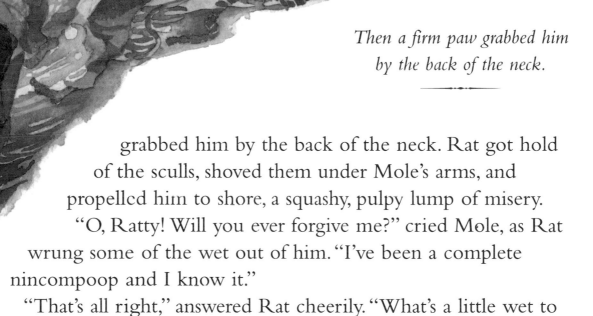

*Then a firm paw grabbed him
by the back of the neck.*

grabbed him by the back of the neck. Rat got hold
of the sculls, shoved them under Mole's arms, and
propelled him to shore, a squashy, pulpy lump of misery.

"O, Ratty! Will you ever forgive me?" cried Mole, as Rat
wrung some of the wet out of him. "I've been a complete
nincompoop and I know it."

"That's all right," answered Rat cheerily. "What's a little wet to
a water rat? But I do think you had better come and stop with me
for a time. I'll teach you to row, and to swim, and you'll soon be as
handy on the water as any of us."

And that's just what they did. Mole learnt to swim and to row
and each day seemed longer and more full of interest as the ripening
summer moved onward.

The Open Road

ONE BRIGHT SUMMER MORNING, Rat was sitting on the riverbank singing a song about ducks which he had just composed when Mole interrupted him.

"I wanted to ask you, Ratty," said Mole, "if we could visit Mr Toad. I've heard so much about him."

"Why certainly," said Rat. "Get the boat out and we'll paddle up there now."

As soon as the boat was ready, Mole took the sculls and off they went. Rounding a bend in the river, they came in sight of a handsome, red-brick house with well-kept lawns sweeping down to the water's edge.

"There's Toad Hall," said Rat. "Toad is rather rich, you know, and this is one of the nicest houses in these parts, though we never tell Toad that."

"Toad is rather rich, you know, and this is one of the nicest houses in these parts."

They disembarked and strolled across the lawns, where they found Toad resting in a garden chair, a large map spread out across his knees.

"Hooray!" he cried, jumping up. "I was just going to send a boat down to fetch you, Ratty. I want you badly – both of you."

"It's about your rowing, I suppose," said Rat.

"O, pooh! Boating!" interrupted Toad in great disgust. "No, I've discovered the real thing, the only thing. Come with me and see!"

He led the way to the coach-house. Outside stood a canary-yellow gipsy caravan, shining with newness.

"There's real life for you," cried Toad, "in that cart! The open road, the hedgerows, the rolling downs! Here today, there tomorrow. You'll find every comfort inside, and we make our start this afternoon."

"I beg your pardon," said Rat slowly, "but did I hear you say something about 'we' and 'start' and 'this afternoon'?"

"Now, Ratty," said Toad imploringly, "don't talk in that sniffy way. I can't manage without you, so don't argue."

"I'm not coming," said Rat. "And Mole's not coming either, are you, Mole?"

"Let's discuss it over lunch," said Toad, quickly.

Lunch was excellent, of course, and Toad persuasive, and Rat at last agreed to go.

Outside stood a canary-yellow gipsy caravan, shining with newness.

Toad sent Rat and Mole out to catch the old grey horse, while he packed the caravan with even more things. At last they were away, and by late evening they were miles from home. They drew up on a common, turned the horse loose to graze, and ate their supper on the grass. When they settled into their little bunks for the night, Toad said sleepily, "This is the real life for a gentleman!"

No amount of shaking would wake him next morning, so Rat and Mole were left to feed the horse, light a fire, make breakfast and shop for things that Toad had forgotten. By the time Toad appeared, they were exhausted.

They had a pleasant ramble that day and camped as before, on a common. Rat made sure that Toad did his share of work, so that when it was time to set off next morning, Toad wasn't quite as thrilled with his new life.

In the afternoon, disaster struck. The friends were strolling along a high road when they heard a distant hum. They glanced back to see a small cloud of dust coming towards them at incredible speed. In an instant, a blast of wind and sound made them jump for the nearest ditch. A loud *poop-poop* assaulted their ears, just as they glimpsed a magnificent motor-car before it enveloped them in dust and sped off. The horse reared, there was a heartrending crash - and the canary-coloured cart lay wrecked on its side in a deep ditch.

Rat danced up and down in the road yelling, "Villains, road-hogs," while Mole tried to calm the horse. Toad sat down in the middle of the road, and murmured *poop-poop*. "Glorious sight!" he continued. "The real way to travel! The only way to

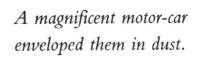

A magnificent motor-car enveloped them in dust.

travel. O bliss! O poop-poop!"

"O stop being an idiot, Toad!" cried Mole.

"And to think I never knew!" went on Toad. "But now – what carts I shall fling into the ditch! Horrid little carts – canary-coloured carts!"

"What are we going to do with him?" asked Mole.

"Nothing," replied Rat. "He is in the grip of a new craze. There is nothing to be done."

Like many people, Toad had never seen a motor-car before. Cars then were an unusual sight because only the rich could afford to own them.

The Wild Wood

FOR A LONG TIME Mole had wanted to meet Badger. From what he had heard, he seemed such an important and influential animal. But whenever Mole mentioned his wish to Rat, he found himself being fobbed off. "Badger'll turn up some day," Rat would say.

The summer rolled on, with plenty to do each day. But when winter came, and Rat spent a lot of the time asleep, Mole found himself thinking about Badger again. One afternoon, when Rat was dozing in his armchair, Mole came to a decision. He slipped out through the door, and set off towards the Wild Wood.

Mole was alone, far from any help; and the night was closing in.

There was nothing to frighten him as he took his first steps into the wood. But deeper inside, it grew darker and everything was still. Then the faces began. Over his shoulder he thought he saw an evil wedge-shaped face looking out at him from a hole. He quickened his pace. He passed another hole, and another, and then – a little narrow face flashed up from a hole, and was gone. Then suddenly, every hole seemed to frame a face, each one staring at him all hard-eyed and evil, before disappearing.

Then the whistling began. Very faint and shrill at first but soon it seemed to travel the whole length and breadth of the wood. They were up and ready, whoever they were! And he – Mole – was alone, far from any help; and the night was closing in.

Then the pattering began. Mole knew it could only be the pat-pat-pat of little feet. It grew until the whole wood seemed to be chasing, closing in round something – or somebody. Mole began to run. He ran into things, he darted under things and dodged round things. At last he took refuge in the dark deep hollow of an old beech tree. As he tried to make himself comfortable in the dry leaves and hoped he was safe, he knew what Rat and other dwellers of the field and hedgerow had encountered – the Terror of the Wild Wood!

Rat set off to find Mole.

When Rat woke and discovered Mole's tracks heading for the Wild Wood, he took a pair of pistols and set off to find him. Little faces popped out of holes, but vanished at the sight of brave Rat with his weapons. The whistling and pattering started up but soon died away. Rat left the paths and fought his way across the Wood, calling out cheerfully, "Moly, Moly, Moly! Where are you?"

It was another hour before he heard a feeble voice calling from the hollow of an old beech tree, and found Mole, exhausted and still trembling. "O Rat!" cried Mole. "I've been so frightened."

"You shouldn't have come here, Mole," said Rat soothingly. "There are a hundred and one passwords and signs you need to know." Rat chattered on, and Mole soon began to feel more himself. But when they were ready to set off for home, they found it was snowing hard. "Well," said Rat after pondering for a while, "we must make a start. The trouble is, I don't quite know where we are."

An hour or two later, aching with tiredness, they gave up, and struggled down into a dell for shelter. Suddenly, Mole tripped and fell on his face with a squeal. "O, my poor shin!" he cried.

"Poor old chap," said Rat. He examined Mole's leg carefully. "Looks as if this cut was made by a sharp edge of something metal." He began to scratch around in the snow. After a few moments he cried, "Hooray! Come and see!"

Mole hobbled over and said, "I see a door-scraper. What of it?"

"But don't you see what it means," cried Rat impatiently.

"It means that some very careless creature has left his door-scraper lying about just where it's sure to trip everybody up!" complained Mole.

Rat had begun to dig again. Soon, he uncovered a very shabby doormat.

"There!" he cried triumphantly. "What does that tell you?"

"Whoever heard of a doormat telling you anything?" sulked Mole.

"Now look here, you - you dolt," replied Rat angrily, "just dig if you want to sleep in a warm bed tonight."

Mole did as he was told, even though he thought Rat was behaving very oddly. Ten minutes later, Rat uncovered a solid-looking, dark green door. On a small brass plate below a bell-pull, they read: MR BADGER. Mole fell backwards in the snow. "Rat!" he cried, "you're a wonder! From the moment you found that door-scraper you worked it out all by yourself. If only I had your head, Ratty –"

"But as you haven't," said Rat rather unkindly, "hang on to that bell-pull and ring as hard as you can!"

Mole fell backwards in the snow. "Rat!" he cried, "you're a wonder!"

At last they heard the sound of slow shuffling footsteps, followed by the noise of a bolt being shot back. The door opened a few inches to show a long snout and a pair of sleepy blinking eyes.

"Who is it, disturbing people at this time of night?" said a gruff voice. "Speak up!"

"It's me, Rat, and my friend Mole. We've lost our way in the snow."

"Why, Ratty!" exclaimed Badger. "Come in at once, both of you, you must be perished. Well I never! Lost in the snow! In the Wild Wood, at this time of night!"

The two animals tumbled over each other in their eagerness to get inside. Badger patted their heads, and led them down a long, gloomy and rather shabby passage into the glow and warmth of a large kitchen. He thrust them

They gathered round the glowing embers of the fire, feeling happy and full.

down on a bench to toast themselves in front of the fire, while he bustled about fetching dressing gowns and slippers and bathing Mole's shin.

When at last Rat and Mole were thoroughly toasted, they tucked in hungrily to the supper Badger had prepared, and told the story of their adventures in the Wild Wood. Then they gathered round the glowing embers of the great wood fire, feeling happy and full.

Badgers hibernate, or go to sleep, through the winter. This is why Badger cannot help Toad until the spring.

"Tell us the news from your part of the world," said Badger heartily. "How's old Toad getting on?"

"O, from bad to worse," said Rat gravely. "Another smash-up only last week, and a bad one. He will insist on driving himself, thinks he's a heaven-born driver, but he's absolutely hopeless."

"How many has he had?" asked Badger.

"Smashes, or machines?" asked Rat. "O, well, it's the same thing with Toad. This is the seventh. His coach-house is piled up to the roof with bits of motor-cars."

"He's been in hospital three times," said Mole. "As for the fines he's had to pay —"

"At this rate he'll either be killed or ruined," continued Rat. "Badger, we're his friends, shouldn't we do something?"

Badger thought very hard and then said, "Well, of course I can't do anything now, in the middle of winter, but once the summer comes, then we'll take Toad seriously in hand. Right now, it's time we were all in bed."

Home Sweet Home

RAT AND MOLE were returning from a long day's exploring with Otter. The light was fading and the sting of frozen sleet reminded them that they were cold and tired and that Rat's house was a weary way away.

They plodded along steadily, when suddenly Mole stopped in his tracks. Something was calling him, something stirred and tickled and thrilled his senses. His nose twitched as he tried to grasp its meaning. Another moment, and a rush of old memories came flooding back.

"Ratty!" he called, full of excitement. "Please stop, Ratty! It's my old home! I've just come across the smell of it. I must go to it, I must, I must!"

Rat was too far ahead of Mole to hear what he was saying.

"Mole, we daren't stop," he called back. "It's late and it's going to snow." He hurried on without waiting for an answer. Mole stood alone in the road, a big sob welling up inside him. With a wrench that tore at his heart-strings, he set off down the road after Rat.

At last, when they had gone quite a distance further, Rat gazed at Mole and said kindly, "Mole, old chap, you look all in. Let's sit down and rest for a minute."

No sooner had Mole sat down than he began to sob uncontrollably. Rat looked on with astonishment and dismay. "What is it, old fellow?" he said gently.

"I know it's a – shabby little place," choked Mole in between sobs, "but it was my own little home – and I was fond of it – and I smelt it suddenly back there – and I wanted it – but you wouldn't turn back, Ratty, you wouldn't turn back!"

"What a pig I've been!" said Rat, patting Mole gently on the shoulder.

"Well, we're going to find that home of yours, if I have to stay out all night."

Still snuffling, Mole let himself be dragged back along the road by his determined friend. When at last it seemed they must be near, Rat said cheerfully, "Now, Mole, use that nose of yours to sniff your way home." They moved on in silence, then Mole stood rigid for a moment and twitched his whiskers. With something of the air of a sleep-walker, he crossed a dry ditch, scrambled through a hedge, and sniffed his way across a field. Suddenly, without any warning, he dived. Rat scrabbled behind, down a long, narrow tunnel, until at last there was room enough for him to stand upright again. Mole struck a match. Directly facing them was his little front door, with "Mole End" painted over the bell-pull.

"What a pig I've been!"
said Rat, patting Mole
gently on the shoulder.

Once inside, Mole glanced round his old home. He saw the dust lying thick on its worn contents, and collapsed on a chair. "O, Ratty," he cried. "Why did I bring you to this cold little place, when you could have been at River Bank warming your toes by the fire?"

Rat, though, was running around inspecting rooms and lighting lamps. "What a delightful house!" he said cheerily. "So neat and well planned. We'll make a jolly good night of it. Bustle about, old chap!"

Encouraged by his friend, Mole dusted and polished while Rat soon had a blaze roaring up the chimney. But suddenly, Mole buried his face in his duster. "Ratty," he moaned, "what about supper? I've nothing to give you!"

"We'll find something," said Rat. "Come and help me look."

They hunted and found a tin of sardines, a box of biscuits and a German sausage. "A banquet!" observed Rat.

They were just about to tuck in to supper, when they heard muffled voices outside. "It's the fieldmice!" exclaimed Mole. "They always go carol singing at this time of year, and they save Mole End till last because I always give them supper."

Rat jumped up and ran to the door. By the dim rays of a lantern stood ten little fieldmice. Their shrill little voices launched into an old-time carol. Finally Rat cried, "Well sung, boys. Now come along in and warm up by the fire."

"This is just like old times," cried Mole. But then he yelped in despair. "O, Ratty, we haven't got anything to give them!"

"Leave it to me," said Ratty. He gave one of the fieldmice a coin and a

Traditionally, carol singers are offered mince-pies or money for charity in return for their singing. The fieldmice are lucky to have a whole meal!

large basket and sent him out through the door. The fieldmouse soon returned laden with delicious food. Mole saw his little friends' faces beam as they tucked in, and he couldn't help thinking what a happy home-coming this had turned out to be after all.

By the dim rays of a lantern stood ten little fieldmice.

Mr Toad

ONE BRIGHT SUMMER MORNING, Rat and Mole were eating breakfast when there was a loud knock at the door. Mole answered it with a cry of surprise and Badger strode into the room.

"The hour of Toad has come!" he proclaimed. "Another new car is due to arrive at Toad Hall this morning. You two will accompany me to take that animal in hand."

They arrived at Toad Hall to find a huge red car standing outside the house, and Toad swaggering down the steps, dressed in goggles, cap and an enormous overcoat. "Hullo!" he

cried. "You're just in time to come for a jolly –" He stopped as Badger strode up the steps and pushed him back inside.

"Now then," said Badger sternly, "first of all, take off those ridiculous clothes."

"Shan't!" replied Toad, with great spirit.

"Take them off him, you two," ordered Badger.

They had to lay Toad out kicking on the floor before they could even begin to remove his finery.

"You knew it would come to this, Toad," said Badger. "You've ignored all our warnings and you're getting us animals a bad name.

Toad swaggered down the steps, dressed in goggles, cap and an enormous overcoat.

Come with me into the library."

"That's no good," said Rat contemptuously after they'd gone. "Talking to Toad'll never cure him, he'll say anything."

Some three-quarters of an hour later, the library door opened and Badger reappeared, leading by the paw a very limp and sorrowful Toad.

"Sit down, Toad," said Badger kindly. "Now, I want you to repeat before your friends what you promised me just now: that you are sorry for your bad conduct, that you see the foolishness of it all, and that you will give up cars for good."

There was a long pause while Toad looked desperately from one animal to the other. At last he spoke. "I'm not sorry. And it wasn't foolishness at all! It was simply wonderful!"

"You back-sliding animal!" cried Badger. "You told me in there —"

"O, yes, in there," said Toad. "I'd have said anything in there. But I've been searching my mind since and I'm not sorry, so there's no point in saying I am, is there?"

"Very well, then," said Badger. "Perhaps a spell locked in your room will help you see the error of your ways. Take him up, you two."

"Toad must be guarded at all times," said Badger. "We must take it in turns to be with him until he has come to his senses."

They arranged watches accordingly. Each animal took it in turns to sleep in Toad's room at night, and they divided the day up between them. At first, Toad made life very difficult for them. He would arrange chairs in the shape of a car, crouch on the one at the front, lean forward staring straight ahead, and make the most ghastly noises. Then he would turn a complete somersault, falling flat on the floor amongst the ruins of the chairs, apparently completely satisfied for the time being. These moments of madness grew gradually less frequent, and his friends tried to interest him in other things. But Toad became listless and depressed.

One fine morning it was Rat's turn to go on duty. "Be very careful, Rat," warned Badger on his way out. "When Toad's quiet and obedient, he's at his craftiest."

"How are you today, old chap?" asked Rat cheerfully, as he approached Toad's bedside.

He had to wait some minutes for an answer. At last a feeble voice replied, "Dear, kind Rat, do not trouble about me. I hate being a burden to my friends, and I do not expect to be one much longer."

It was common for people to ask for lawyers to be present at their deathbed to write their will. Toad wants Rat to think he's very ill.

"I'm glad to hear it's going to stop," said Rat heartily. "I'd take any trouble on earth for you if only you'd be a sensible animal."

"Then I beg you," said Toad, more feebly than ever, "to fetch the doctor."

"What do you want a doctor for?" said Rat, beginning to feel worried. Toad certainly lay still and flat and seemed out of sorts.

"And would you mind, at the same time, fetching my lawyer –

I hate to be a nuisance, but there is a moment when one must face such disagreeable tasks."

"O, he must be really bad!" said the frightened Rat, and he hurried from the room, locking the door behind him, and ran off to the village.

Toad darted to the window as soon as he heard the key turn in the lock, and watched Rat disappear down the drive. Then, laughing fit to burst, he dressed in his smartest suit, knotted the sheets from his bed together, tied one end fast, scrambled out of the window and slid lightly down to the ground. He took the opposite direction to Rat and swaggered off, whistling a merry tune.

Toad scrambled out of the window and slid lightly down to the ground.

As soon as he felt safe from recapture, Toad left the fields and almost danced along the highroad. "Poor old Ratty!" he chuckled. "Won't he catch it when Badger gets back!"

He swaggered along until he reached a little town, where he strode into an inn and ordered the best lunch on the menu. He was about halfway through his meal when he heard a car drawing up outside the inn. Its owners came into the room and talked loudly about their wonderful machine, until Toad could stand it no longer. He paid his bill and slipped quietly out. "There can't be any harm," he said to himself, "in just looking!"

The car stood in the middle of the yard. "I wonder if this sort of car starts easily?" he said to himself. Next moment, he had hold of the handle and was turning it. The engine roared into life and the old passion seized Toad. As if in a dream, he found himself seated in the driver's seat. He put his foot down, flew on to the high road out into the open country, and was conscious only that he was Toad once more, Toad at his most majestic...

"The hardened ruffian we see cowering in the dock," said the Magistrate, "has been found guilty of stealing

"It's going to be twenty years for you this time. Take him away."

a valuable motor-car, of reckless driving, and of gross insolence to the police. What is the stiffest penalty we can impose for each of these offences?"

The Clerk of the Court scratched his nose. "Supposing you were to say twelve months for the theft, three years for the reckless driving and fifteen years for cheeking the police. That comes to nineteen years, so make it a round twenty to be on the safe side."

"Excellent!" said the Chairman. "Prisoner! Stand up straight. It's going to be twenty years for you this time. Take him away."

Poor Toad was loaded with chains, and dragged shrieking from the Court House until they reached the grimmest dungeon in the heart of the innermost keep. The rusty key creaked in the lock, the great door clanged behind them; and Toad was a helpless prisoner.

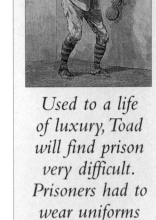

Used to a life of luxury, Toad will find prison very difficult. Prisoners had to wear uniforms and spend long hours hard at work.

For several weeks, Toad refused to eat. "This is the end of the career of the popular and handsome Toad!" he cried from his stinking dungeon. But the gaoler's daughter felt sorry for him. One morning, she said, "Listen, Toad, I have an aunt who is a washerwoman."

"I have several aunts who ought to be washerwomen," said Toad.

"Shhh," said the gaoler's daughter. "My aunt does the washing for all the prisoners in this castle. I am sure that if you paid her well, she would let you have her clothes and you could escape from here as the official washerwoman."

"Surely you wouldn't want Mr Toad, of Toad Hall, going about the country disguised as a washerwoman!" cried Toad, huffily.

"Then you can stop here as a Toad," replied the girl.

Toad quickly changed his tune and agreed to the plan.

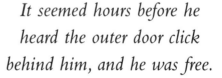

It seemed hours before he heard the outer door click behind him, and he was free.

The very next evening, the girl ushered her aunt into Toad's cell. In return for a few gold coins, Toad received a dress, an apron, a shawl and an old black bonnet. With a quaking heart, he set off down the corridors of the prison, but was surprised to find that nobody questioned the washerwoman's squat figure and every barred door and gateway opened for him. Even so, it seemed hours before he heard the outer door click behind him, and he was free.

He had no idea what to do next, except that he had to get away, and so he walked quickly towards the lights of a town. Soon, his

attention was caught by the sound of
the snorting of engines.

"What luck!" he thought. "A
railway-station!" But when Toad
reached the booking-office, he
remembered to his horror that he had
left his money in his cell. He
wandered down the platform where
his train was standing, tears trickling
down his nose. Very soon, his escape
would be discovered, he would be
caught, loaded with chains, and dragged back to prison again.

*Steam engines were noisy
and dirty. The engine-driver's
shirts would have been filthy
from all the smoke and coal
used to fuel the train.*

Suddenly, a voice called, "Hello, mother! What's the trouble?"
Toad looked up to see the burly engine-driver. "O, sir," he cried.
"I'm a poor unhappy washerwoman, and I've lost all my
money, and I can't pay for my ticket, and I must get home
tonight for my children!"

"Well," said the engine-driver, "if you'll wash
a few shirts for me when you get home, I'll
give you a ride on my engine."

Toad's misery turned to joy as he
clambered up into the cab of the
engine. He'd never washed a shirt in
his life, but once he was home he
could send the engine-driver
enough money to pay for a whole
pile of washing to be done.

*"I'm a poor unhappy
washerwoman, and I've lost
all my money..."*

They had covered many a mile, when the engine-driver suddenly cried, "There's another train following us! The engine is crowded with policemen waving revolvers and shouting –"

"Stop, stop!" Toad fell on his knees and begged, "Save me, dear kind Mr Engine-driver, and I will confess everything! I'm not a washerwoman, I'm the well-known and popular Toad. I have just escaped from a loathsome dungeon."

The engine-driver looked at him sternly. "What were you put in prison for?"

"Nothing much," said Toad. "I borrowed a motor-car while the owners were at lunch, but I didn't mean to steal it."

"I ought to give you up," said the engine-driver, "but I don't like being ordered around

"There's another train following us!"
cried the engine-driver.

by police-men when I'm on my own engine. So I'll do my best for you."

They leaped full steam ahead, but the other engine was faster. The engine-driver wiped his brow and said, "Your only chance is to jump out into the woods once we have passed through that long tunnel ahead." They piled on more coals and the train shot into the tunnel. When they shot out at the other end, the driver put on the brakes. Toad got down on the steps, and as the train slowed down to almost a walking pace, he jumped.

He rolled down an embankment, scrambled into the wood, and
hid. Peeping out, he saw his train gather speed again and disappear at
a great pace. Then out of the tunnel burst the other engine, her
crew waving their weapons and shouting, "Stop, stop, stop!"

When they were past, Toad laughed until his sides were splitting.
But he soon stopped when he realised that it was dark and cold and
he was still far from friends and home. He dared not leave the shelter
of the trees, so he struck off into the wood, with the idea of leaving
the railway as far behind him as possible.
At last, cold, hungry, and tired out,
he found a hollow tree, where he
made himself as comfortable
as possible and slept till
the morning.

Toad set off early the next morning and soon came to a canal, where a shire horse was pulling a barge. "Nice morning, ma'am!" called the barge-woman as she drew level with Toad.

"Not for me," cried Toad. "I'm supposed to be going to Toad Hall to wash for the distinguished gentleman who lives there, but I've lost my money and my way!"

"Toad Hall?" said the barge-woman. "It's on my way. I'll give you a lift."

Toad thanked her kindly, and stepped on board chuckling happily to himself.

"So you're in the washing business, ma'am," said the barge-woman politely. "What luck! I've a pile of washing waiting to be done, so you can do it for me!"

"Ugh!" cried the barge-woman. "A horrid, crawly Toad!"

Toad tried to protest, but saw that he was cornered. "I suppose any fool can wash!" he thought to himself, and set to work. When he lost the soap for the fiftieth time, loud laughter made him look round.

"Washerwoman, my foot!" gasped the barge-woman. "You've never so much as washed a dishcloth in your life!"

"You common, low, fat barge-woman!" shouted Toad. "I'll have you know that I am Toad of Toad Hall, and I will not be laughed at by a barge-woman!"

"Ugh!" cried the barge-woman. "A horrid, crawly Toad!" And she shoved him into the canal. Thirsting for revenge, he struggled ashore, caught up with the horse, unfastened the ropes, and galloped away in triumph.

Some miles further on, after he had sold the horse to a gipsy in return for breakfast, Toad reached a high road and heard a familiar 'Poop, poop!' His heart raced as a car came zooming towards him. He sank into a sad heap in the road. "O hapless Toad!" he cried. But the occupants, thinking he was a washerwoman who had fainted, carried him into the car and continued on their way.

After a while, knowing that he had not been recognised, Toad asked to be allowed to try driving the car. With much amusement, the driver changed places and Toad set off cautiously. Then he went a little faster; then faster still, and faster. "Be careful, washerwoman!" cried the driver.

"Washerwoman, indeed!" shouted Toad recklessly. "I am Toad, the car-snatcher, the prison-breaker!"

They tried to grab him but Toad turned the wheel and the car went crashing through a hedge. Toad flew through the air, and landed with a splash in the river. He rose to the surface and grabbed at the reeds that grew along the water's edge, but the stream was too strong and he was pulled under again. He rose breathless and spluttering and grabbed at a hole in the bank. As he hung there panting, he saw something twinkling inside. A face grew up round it, brown and small, with whiskers. It was Ratty!

Toad flew through the air, and landed with a splash in the river.

The Fight for Toad Hall

RAT HOISTED THE WATER-LOGGED TOAD into his hall. "Go upstairs," he said, "take off that cotton rag that looks as if it might have belonged to a washerwoman, and try to come down looking respectable." Toad was about to argue, but caught sight of himself in a mirror and did as he was told.

When he came down again, lunch was on the table. He ate hungrily and began to boast about his adventures. When at last he had talked himself to a standstill, Rat said, "Toady, you've been making a prize fool of yourself. You've been handcuffed, imprisoned, starved, chased, terrified out of your life, insulted and jeered at. Where's the fun in that?" Toad was itching to say, "But it was fun!" Yet when Rat had finished, he sighed and said, "Quite right, Ratty! I've been a fool, but from now on I'm going to be good. I'll stroll gently down to Toad Hall and begin to lead a quiet and respectable life."

"But Toady," cried Rat. "When you were – taken away – after that bit of – trouble – and while Mole and Badger were very kindly house-sitting for you, the Wild Wooders broke into Toad Hall, turfed poor Mole and Badger out, and have been living there ever since. They're telling everybody that they're staying for good."

"O, are they?" cried Toad. "I'll jolly soon see about that!"

"No you won't," said Ratty. "You'll stay here until Mole and Badger come back from patrolling round your house and planning how to get it back for you."

Mole and Badger didn't return until after supper. Mole was delighted to see Toad and couldn't wait to hear about his adventures. Badger wouldn't speak until he had eaten, then he said

Rat hoisted the water-logged Toad into his hall.

Grand houses, like Toad Hall, often had secret passageways. The owners could hide from their enemies in times of trouble.

severely, "Toad! You bad, troublesome animal! Aren't you ashamed of yourself? What would your father have said if he had known of all your goings-on?" He softened when Toad began to sob, but then told them all to listen. "I'm going to tell you a secret, told to me by your father, Toad. There is an underground passage that leads from the riverbank quite near here, right up into the middle of Toad Hall."

"O, nonsense! Badger," said Toad. "I know every inch of Toad Hall, inside and out. There's nothing of the sort, I do assure you."

"It leads right up under the butler's pantry, next to the dining hall," insisted Badger, "where, tomorrow night, all the weasels will be gathered together for a big banquet, so I hear."

"We'll creep out quietly into the butler's pantry –" cried Mole.

"– with our pistols and swords and sticks –" shouted Rat.

"– and rush in upon them," said Badger.

"– and whack 'em, and whack 'em, and whack 'em!" cried Toad.

"Our plan is settled then," said Badger. "And now it's time we went to bed."

Mole was delighted to see Toad and couldn't wait to hear about his adventures.

What a squealing and a screeching filled the air!

When it began to grow dark the next day, Rat issued his friends with pistols and swords and sticks, together with handcuffs and bandages. Badger took a lantern in one paw, grasped his great stick with the other, and said, "Now then, follow me!"

He led them along by the river for a little way, then suddenly swung himself over the edge into a hole in the bank. There they were, in the secret passage! It was cold and dark. Soon, Toad was seized with terror and lurched forward so quickly that he knocked into Rat, who knocked into Mole, who knocked into Badger, who nearly drew his pistol on Toad in the confusion. Badger was so angry he threatened to send Toad back. They shuffled along, ears pricked up, until they heard sounds of cheering close by.

They hurried on until the end of the passage, and they found themselves standing under a trap-door. "Now, boys," said Badger, "all together!" They heaved back the trap-door and scrambled up into the pantry. Right next door, the Chief Weasel could be heard making a rather rude speech about Toad.

"Let me get at him!" muttered Toad.

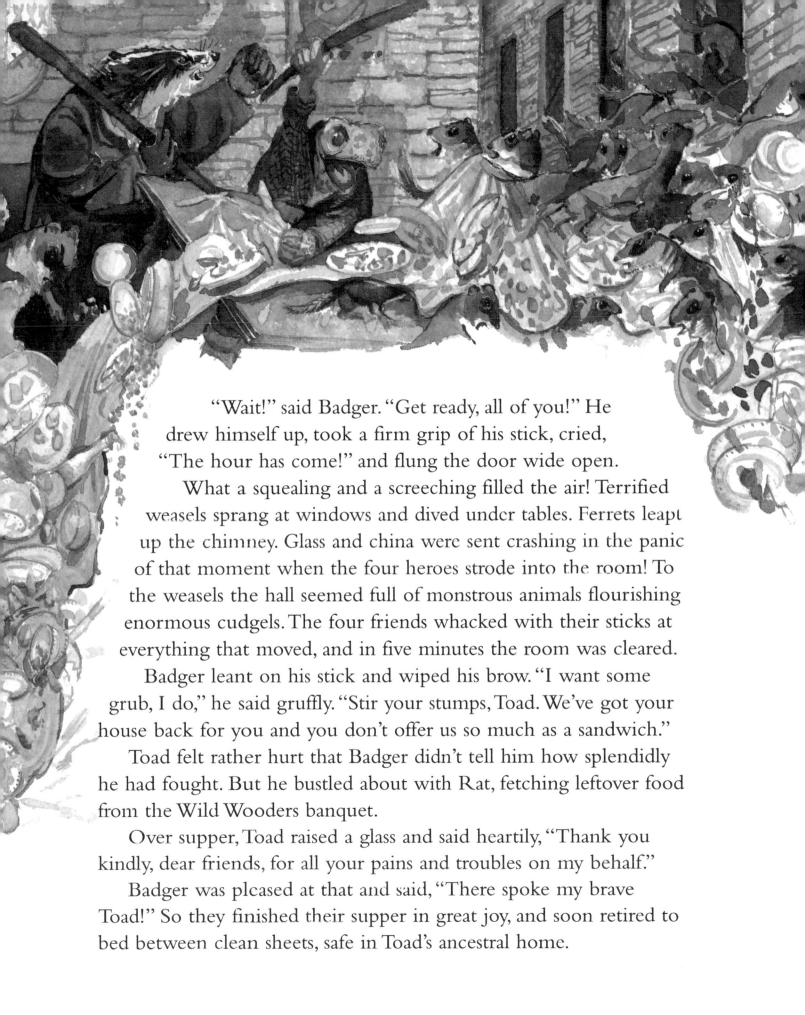

"Wait!" said Badger. "Get ready, all of you!" He drew himself up, took a firm grip of his stick, cried, "The hour has come!" and flung the door wide open.

What a squealing and a screeching filled the air! Terrified weasels sprang at windows and dived under tables. Ferrets leapt up the chimney. Glass and china were sent crashing in the panic of that moment when the four heroes strode into the room! To the weasels the hall seemed full of monstrous animals flourishing enormous cudgels. The four friends whacked with their sticks at everything that moved, and in five minutes the room was cleared.

Badger leant on his stick and wiped his brow. "I want some grub, I do," he said gruffly. "Stir your stumps, Toad. We've got your house back for you and you don't offer us so much as a sandwich."

Toad felt rather hurt that Badger didn't tell him how splendidly he had fought. But he bustled about with Rat, fetching leftover food from the Wild Wooders banquet.

Over supper, Toad raised a glass and said heartily, "Thank you kindly, dear friends, for all your pains and troubles on my behalf."

Badger was pleased at that and said, "There spoke my brave Toad!" So they finished their supper in great joy, and soon retired to bed between clean sheets, safe in Toad's ancestral home.

The following morning, Toad came down to breakfast disgracefully late to be told by Badger that he had work to do. "You see," said Badger, "we must have a banquet to celebrate all that's happened. You must write invitations to all our friends," said Badger.

"Meanwhile, I'll order the banquet."

"What!" cried Toad. "Me stop indoors and write a lot of rotten letters when I want to go round my property and set everything to rights! Certainly not! I'll be –" Toad suddenly changed his tone and agreed with Badger. Then he left the room, went to

He would write the invitations, and he would make sure everybody knew about his triumphant adventures.

the kitchen, and closed the door behind him. A fine idea had occurred to him. He would write the invitations, and he would make sure everybody knew about his triumphant adventures.

By the time the others came back to lunch, Toad had finished and was swaggering about. Rat and Badger were very suspicious.

Great feasts, or banquets, like Toad's were a popular way of entertaining friends and celebrating important events.

"Now, look here, Toad," said Rat. "About this Banquet. There are going to be no speeches, and no songs."

"Not even one little song?" pleaded Toad, his pleasant dream shattered.

"Not one," replied Rat. "Your songs and your speeches are all boasting. It's time for you to turn over a new leaf."

Toad nodded his head sadly and retired to his bedroom. But as the hour of the Banquet drew near, a smile spread across his face. He arranged some chairs in a semicircle, stood in front of them, and began to sing about his adventures to his imaginary audience. When he had finished, he heaved a sigh and went down to greet his guests.

All the animals cheered when he entered and complimented him on his cleverness and courage. Toad only smiled faintly and murmured, "Badger was the mastermind," and "I only served in the ranks." The animals were very puzzled by this unexpected attitude, and Toad felt that he was an object of absorbing interest to everyone.

The Banquet was a great success. There was much talking and laughter among the animals, but through it all Toad quietly murmured pleasant nothings to those on either side of him. From time to time, he stole a glance at Badger and Rat and saw them staring at each other in astonishment, and this gave him great satisfaction. Even when there were cries of "Toad! Speech! Song!" Toad shook his head gently and managed to convey to everyone that these were a thing of the past. Hc was indeed an altered Toad!

The Banquet was
a great success.

Life Along the Riverbank

KENNETH GRAHAME loved walking by the river and knew all about the real animals and insects that lived there. He included many of them in *The Wind in the Willows*. In the story he gives the animals human characteristics based on his observation of real animals.

Animals are not the only ones to enjoy life by the river. Many people spend their time here too, although most of the animals keep well away from them.

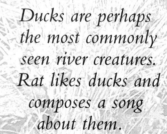

❀ MOLE
In the story, Mole is a timid, humble character with an obstinate streak! In real life, moles are small and quiet, but need strength and determination for digging tunnels.

Ducks are perhaps the most commonly seen river creatures. Rat likes ducks and composes a song about them.

❀ TOAD
Toad's boastful nature is probably based on a toad's ability to puff itself up and croak loudly. This makes it seem more important than it really is.

✾ OTTER

Otter is a kindly fellow who pops up at unexpected times to say hello to Rat and Mole. You would be lucky to spot an otter in real life as they live in well-hidden dens or "holts" in the riverbank.

✾ WATER RAT

As in the story, the water rat, or vole, spends a great deal of time in the river, and lives in a burrow or hole in the riverbank.

The beauty of the dragonfly as it speeds along adds to the enchantment of the water's surface.

✾ WOODLAND ANIMALS

As Rat explains to Mole, the woodland is home to weasels, stoats, and foxes, and "sometimes they go a bit wild and you can't really trust them." For this reason the riverbankers don't go there much.

Despite being a member of the weasel family, Badger in the story is a trustworthy and strong character.

Mole is frightened by the weasels' "evil wedge-shaped faces" and "hard eyes".

The foxes are one of the main reasons that Toad doesn't like the Wild Wood. Foxes are often portrayed as sly animals.

Kenneth Grahame

KENNETH GRAHAME was born in Scotland, but after his mother died, he went to live with his grandmother in England. His new home was near the River Thames, and it was here that Grahame developed his love of the countryside and of the river.

*Kenneth Grahame
1859–1932*

❀ ALASTAIR

As an adult, like many parents, Grahame made up stories for his son, Alastair. In 1904, he began a bedtime story about a Toad, a Badger, a Water Rat and a Mole. He continued the story in a series of letters to Alastair while he was on holiday.

*Alastair
Grahame*

❀ BANK OF ENGLAND

The story was finally published as *The Wind in the Willows* in 1908. It took a long time to finish because, during the day, Grahame worked at the Bank of England in London.

*Toad in the 1987
television version*

❀ WINDY SUCCESS

The Wind in the Willows was an instant bestseller. However, Grahame refused to write a sequel – especially when, ten years after first publication, his son died. But in 1931 he did allow E. H. Shepard to illustrate the story which has been enduringly popular, along with cartoons, plays, and film versions of the book.

An illustration by Shepard